High-Flying Tea

By Thaddeus Dilday
Illustrated by the Disney Storybook Art Team

A Random House PICTUREBACK® Book
Random House 🏠 New York

Copyright © 2016 Disney Enterprises, Inc. All rights reserved. Published in the United States by Random House Children's Books, a division of Penguin Random House LLC, 1745 Broadway, New York, NY 10019, and in Canada by Penguin Random House Canada Limited, Toronto, in conjunction with Disney Enterprises, Inc. Pictureback, Random House, and the Random House colophon are registered trademarks of Penguin Random House LLC.
randomhousekids.com
ISBN 978-0-7364-3551-2
Printed in the United States of America
10 9 8 7 6 5 4 3 2 1

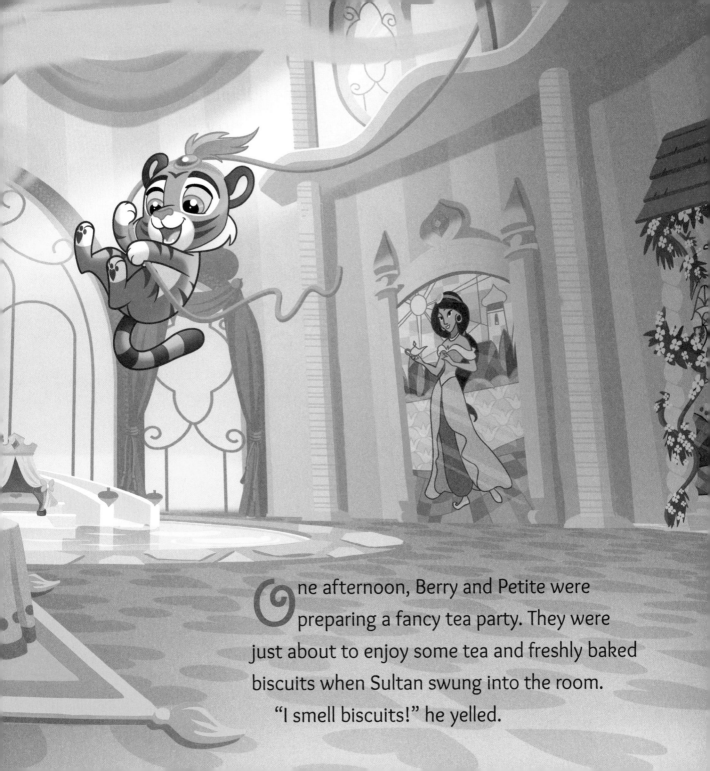

One afternoon, Berry and Petite were preparing a fancy tea party. They were just about to enjoy some tea and freshly baked biscuits when Sultan swung into the room. "I smell biscuits!" he yelled.

"Sorry, Sultan," Berry said. "These biscuits are only for pets who are attending the tea party. That's the rule."

Petite set a heavy book on the table.

"It says so right here in my tea party rule book," she explained.

Sultan looked at the biscuits and licked his lips. He had to have one.

"I can't believe I'm saying this, but can I play tea party with you?" he asked.

Berry was happy to have Sultan join their party—
under one condition: "You have to follow all the rules,"
she warned.

"No problem!" Sultan said confidently.
But Petite and Berry weren't so sure.

At a tea party, fancy attire is a must.
Everyone put on their nicest hats.
Sultan even added a bow tie.

"Okay, I'm all fancy-pantsed up.
Now biscuit me!" he said.

"Tsk, tsk!" scolded
Berry. "The rules say that before
eating, we must make small talk."

Sultan couldn't wait any longer . . . so he pounced!

But Berry whisked the biscuits away just in time.

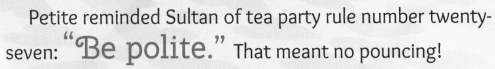

Petite reminded Sultan of tea party rule number twenty-seven: "Be polite." That meant no pouncing!

Sultan apologized. "I meant to say, may I please have a biscuit?"

Berry handed him a biscuit, but before Sultan could take a bite, the bunny exclaimed, "You need a napkin!"

Petite placed a napkin in her lap, and told Sultan that he should do so, too.

Sultan's napkin slid off his lap and a breeze sent it flying across the room. As he raced from the table to get it, Berry and Petite stood up.

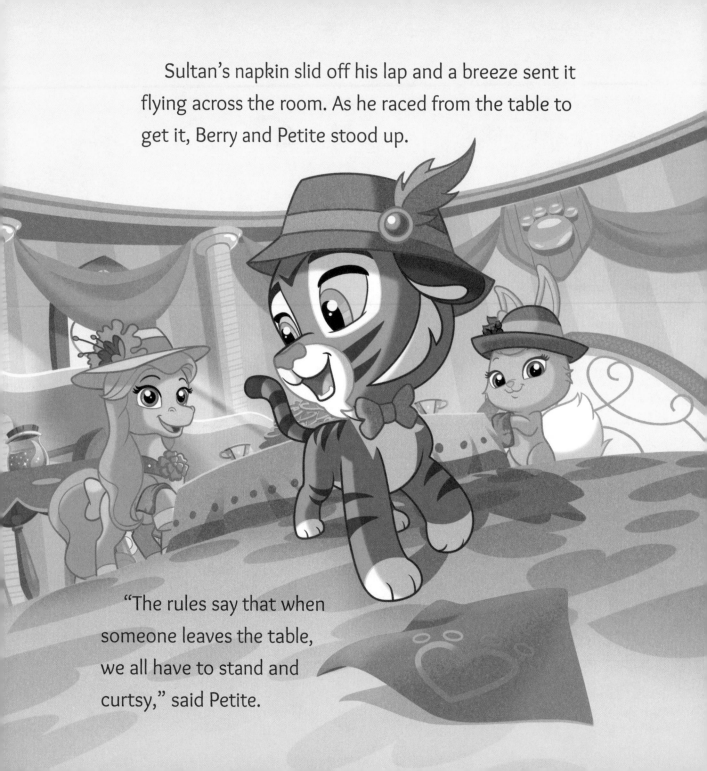

"The rules say that when someone leaves the table, we all have to stand and curtsy," said Petite.

Unfortunately, when Petite curtsied, she accidentally bumped the tea cart, which caused a jar of magical glitterbits to fall onto the rug.

All of a sudden, the carpet swept up Berry and Petite and began to fly! Berry and Petite held on tight as the carpet zoomed around the room.

"Sultan, help!" they cried.

"I would," Sultan called to his friends, "but I don't know the tea party helping rules."

"Forget the rules!" Berry shouted.

Now, **that** was something Sultan could do! He tossed off his hat and bow tie and grabbed a rope from one of the drapes.

Sultan threw the rope like a lasso, catching the carpet just before it flew out the window.

Thankfully, he was able to lower his friends to safety.

"Maybe there's a section in here about dealing with flying carpets," Petite suggested, flipping through her book.

Just then, Sultan had an idea. "Let's have a high-flying tea party!" he said.

The friends went outside and took to the sky, with Sultan safely steering the carpet around Whisker Haven. During the flight, Sultan got to eat as many biscuits as he liked—after all, he had saved the day!